MERCER MAYER'S LC + THE CRITTER KIDS (R)

SHOWDOWN AT THE ARCADE

A Golden Book • New York

Western Publishing Company, Inc., Racine, Wisconsin 53404

A Mercer Mayer Ltd./J. R. Sansevere Book

Library of Congress Catalog Card Number: 93-73740
ISBN: 0-307-15958-2/ISBN: 0-307-65958-5 (lib. bdg.)   A MCMXCIV

Written by Erica Farber/J. R. Sansevere

6075832

LC VELVET LITTLE SIST

TIGER KOOL BEAR SLICK RICK

SU SU

GABBY

TIMOTHY

GATOR

FLEX

HENRIETTA

LC spread some extra chunky peanut butter
and some strawberry jam on a piece of bread and
sprinkled orange juice over it. Then he topped it
off with his favorite ingredient—pickles.

"What is *that*?" Little Sister asked.

"The LC special," LC said. "Want one?"

"No way!" said Little Sister.

4

Mrs. Critter walked into the kitchen. "Hurry, LC, or you'll be late for school," she said. "And don't forget your cookie—it's double chocolate chip marshmallow mint."

LC put the sandwich and the cookie into a paper bag and ran out the door.

"You're late," said Gabby to LC. "I know a shortcut. Follow me."

Gabby ran across her backyard, hopped over a fence, and ran across another backyard to the sidewalk. Just as LC jumped over the fence, Flex, the school bully, walked outside.

"Hey, where are you going?" Flex asked.

"Ummmmm . . ." LC said, "I was just taking a shortcut to school."

"Well, this is my backyard," Flex said. "No trespassing!"

LC hopped back over the fence. Now he was really going to be late for school.

LC got to school just as the last bell rang. He peeked down the hallway to his classroom. The coast was clear. Mrs. Peacock, the principal, was nowhere in sight.

Just then someone tapped him on the shoulder. "Ah, Mr. Critter," said Mrs. Peacock, "I see we

are late for school. Do we have a note?"

LC shook his head. Mrs. Peacock handed him a late slip.

"Two more, and we have detention," she said.

As LC walked to class, he wondered why Mrs. Peacock always said "we." She wasn't the one who was going to end up in detention.

When LC got to his classroom, he handed Mr. Hogwash the late slip.

"Thank you, Mr. Critter," said Mr. Hogwash. "We are on page 34."

LC sat down in his seat and turned his book to page 34. When he looked up, he saw that Gabby had dropped her pencil.

"What happened to you?" Gabby whispered as she picked it up.

"I'll tell you at lunch," said LC.

Just then Tiger handed LC a note.

"Flex told me to give you this," said Tiger. "He said it was important."

LC unfolded the piece of paper. It said, *"Stay out of my way . . . or else!!!"*

Finally it was lunchtime.

"What do you have for lunch?" asked Gabby.

"The LC special," LC said.

"What's that?" asked Gabby.

"A peanut butter and jelly and orange juice and pickles sandwich," LC said. "I've also got a double chocolate chip marshmallow mint cookie."

Flex walked up to the table. "Did I hear someone has a double chocolate chip marshmallow mint cookie?" he asked.

"Yeah, I do," said LC.

"Can I see it?" asked Flex.

LC handed Flex the cookie. Flex took a gigantic bite.

"Thanks," said Flex as he walked away chewing the rest of the cookie.

After school LC, Tiger, Gator, and Gabby went
to shoot hoops. Henrietta, queen of the jam, was
on the court practicing.

"Hey, too bad about your cookie," Henrietta
said as she dunked the ball.

"Yeah," said Tiger as he moved to guard LC.

14

"So, what did Flex's note say?" he asked.

"To stay out of his way," said LC. "And that's what I plan to do."

"Well, don't look now," said Henrietta, "but guess who's coming?"

"Hey, dude, pass the ball," said Flex.

LC threw the ball to Flex. Flex started to dribble. Suddenly there was a loud pop.

"Hey, this ball is bogus!" said Flex. "It doesn't even bounce."

Flex dropped the ball and walked off the court. LC picked up the ball and turned it over. There was a big hole in it. LC looked down. Right by his foot there was a huge nail.

"Flex ruins everything," Gabby said.

Since they couldn't play basketball anymore, LC, Gabby, Tiger, Gator, and Henrietta decided to go to the arcade. LC and Gabby got there first.

"Let's flip for who will be X-Critter," said Gabby.

"Okay," said LC. He took a quarter out of his pocket. Just then someone grabbed the quarter out of LC's hand. It was Flex.

"I'll flip it for you," said Flex. He threw the quarter so high in the air that no one saw it come down.

"Sorry," said Flex. "I'll play while you look for your quarter."

"We've got to have an emergency meeting," Gabby whispered to LC. "We've got to do something about Flex!"

"Order, order, this meeting is now in order," said Gabby. All the Critter Kids sat down around the clubhouse table.

"What's the big idea of calling a meeting on Friday night?"asked Su Su. "I'm going to miss my favorite TV show."

"We have a big problem," said Gabby.

"Problem?" asked Timothy.

"Yes," said Gabby. "And his name is Flex."

20

"What are we going to do?" asked Gator.

"We've got to stand up to him," said Gabby. "And I nominate LC to do it. All those in favor of LC, raise their hands."

Everyone raised their hands.

LC gulped. How was he supposed to stand up to the biggest bully in Critterville . . . or maybe in the whole world?

The next day the Critter Kids were playing
baseball. LC was at bat. As he got ready to swing,
LC heard a familiar voice.

"Hey, let me hit a couple of balls," said Flex.

"We're playing a game," said Gabby.

Flex walked up to LC and put his arm around him. "Come on, dude, I just want to hit a few," said Flex.

LC looked at the ground. "Okay," he said. LC gave Flex the bat and went to the outfield.

Gabby threw her best curve ball. Flex hit it and the ball flew right over LC's head. LC ran as fast as he could, but the ball landed in the swamp. LC knew their ball was gone for good.

That afternoon LC and Gabby took Little Sister to the movies. They stood in line to get a snack.

"What are you going to get?" asked Gabby.

"I'm getting the Chewie Chews," said Little Sister.

"Don't they get stuck in your teeth?" asked Gabby.

"Yeah, that's why I like them," said Little Sister.

Gabby paid for her popcorn. "I'll save you a seat," she said.

LC ordered one box of Chewie Chews and one buttered popcorn. Then he and Little Sister went inside and sat next to Gabby.

"Is that seat empty?" someone asked.

LC couldn't believe his bad luck. It was Flex. On his way to sit down, Flex stepped on LC's foot and knocked over his popcorn.

"Sorry," said Flex. But LC didn't think Flex sounded the teensiest bit sorry.

After the movie LC, Little Sister, and Gabby went to the Critter Cone. They sat at a table in the back.

"Uh-oh," said Gabby. "Here comes Flex."

LC hid behind his menu. He hoped that Flex wouldn't see him.

"Yummy," said Little Sister, taking a big sip of her soda.

Flex walked right up to their table. He sat down and knocked Little Sister's soda out of her hands. It spilled all over her. Little Sister began to cry.

LC started getting mad. "That's it!" he said to Flex. "Step outside."

"Whaddya want?" Flex asked LC.

"I want you to stop picking on everybody," said LC. "That's what."

"Oh, yeah," said Flex. "Who's gonna stop me?"

"I am," said LC. "Next week. Same time. Same

place. The showdown. Be there."

"Okay," said Flex. "May the toughest dude win."

LC gulped. What was he going to do now?

The next morning Gabby woke up LC by blowing a whistle in his ear.

"Rise and shine, LC," said Gabby. "Drop and give me ten."

"Ten what?" asked LC.

"Push-ups," said Gabby.

LC yawned and slowly got out of bed.

"Hustle, hustle," said Gabby. "If you want to beat Flex, you have to be in tip-top condition."

LC dropped to the floor and began his push-ups.

"One, two," said Gabby. "After this, we've got sit-ups, stretching, and then running."

LC sighed. It was going to be a long day.

"Five minutes, forty-six seconds," said Gabby as LC came jogging around the corner. "You've got to pick up your pace."

LC took a deep breath.

"Ready . . . set . . . go!" said Gabby. She clicked the stopwatch.

LC began to run down the block. Tiger came skateboarding toward him.

"Don't talk to him," Gabby yelled at Tiger. "He's in training—every single day this week."

Gabby blew her whistle. "Hit the road, LC," she said. "We have no time to lose."

That afternoon LC and the Critter Kids went to Muscle Beach. Gabby wanted LC to do some weight lifting.

"I'll spot him," said Henrietta.

LC looked up at the sky as Henrietta and Gator lowered the bar into his hands.

"Push, LC!" said Gabby. "All these muscle guys are pumping way more weight than just this bar."

LC pushed as hard as he could, but he couldn't budge the bar. Just then Schwarze-Critter came over to them.

"Why don't you try this?" said Schwarze-Critter. He handed them a wooden broom.

"That's much better," said LC, pumping the broom up and down. Maybe he could beat Flex after all.

After LC finished weight lifting, he and the Critter Kids went to the town gym. Gabby pushed LC over to a punching bag. An old boxer was sitting there.

"Ya gotta give it the old one-two, one-two," the boxer said to LC.

LC started punching the bag. Before he knew what had happened, the bag swung into him and he fell backward onto the floor.

"Don't forget your rhythm," said the boxer. "You gotta get into a rhythm for the KO."

"What's the KO?" asked LC.

"The knockout," said the boxer.

LC's eyes opened wide. He hoped *he* wasn't going to get the KO.

LC followed Gabby's training schedule all week long. The night before the showdown, he was so tired he couldn't even move.

"Are you ready for the showdown?" asked Little Sister.

"I don't know," said LC. "Flex is a lot bigger than me."

"Yeah," said Little Sister.

"And he's a lot tougher than me," said LC.

"Yeah," said Little Sister.

"So I don't know if I can beat him," said LC.

"Yeah," said Little Sister. "Good luck. You're going to need it."

LC tossed and turned, trying to fall asleep. But all he could think about was the showdown and how Flex was going to flatten him in front of all of Critterville.

LC started counting X-Critters to make himself sleepy. The next thing he knew, a gigantic cyborg was coming right for him . . .

"Help!" yelled LC.

"Don't worry," said X-Critter. "Just step on the cyborg's toe."

The cyborg moved closer to LC and aimed a fireball at him. Before the cyborg could shoot, LC stepped on his toe. The cyborg exploded.

"Brainpower is key," said X-Critter. "Use your brain and you'll win . . ."

The next day there was a big crowd outside the Critter Cone. LC walked slowly toward Flex. He kept thinking about what X-Critter had said in his dream. But he still didn't know how using his brain was going to help him beat Flex. LC looked at the arcade. Suddenly he had a great idea.

"What's your highest score in *X-Critter*?" LC asked Flex.

"10,000," said Flex.

"I can beat that," said LC.

"Oh, yeah," said Flex.

"Yeah," said LC. "I challenge you to an
X-Critter match."

"You're just chicken," said Flex.

"I am not," said LC. "If you still want to fight
after we play, then I'll fight. But only if you win
the game."

"Okay," said Flex. "Let's go."

Everyone followed Flex and LC into the arcade.

LC and Flex stood in front of the game.

"I'll be the cyborg," said Flex, hitting a button.

"I'll be X-Critter," said LC, hitting a different button.

Flex banged the control. The cyborg jumped in the air and kicked X-Critter across the screen. 1,000 points flashed on Flex's side.

Before LC could get X-Critter to stand up,

the cyborg grabbed X-Critter and flipped him to the ground for another 1,000 points.

"He's not gonna make it," Gabby whispered to Tiger.

As LC got X-Critter to stand, the cyborg shot a fireball. LC couldn't get X-Critter to duck fast enough. Flex got another 2,000 points.

"One more hit and you're dead!" said Flex.

The cyborg moved slowly toward X-Critter. LC knew he had to think of something fast. As the cyborg got closer, LC realized what he had to do. LC moved X-Critter even closer to the cyborg. Instead of pushing the punch button, he pushed the kick button and hit the cyborg's toe.

The cyborg exploded in a flash of color, just like in his dream. 25,000 points flashed on the screen. LC had won!

"Hey, what happened?" asked Flex. He banged the game with his foot.

"I beat you," said LC.

"Yeah, he beat you," said Gabby. "Fair and square."

"LC, how did you do that?" asked Flex.

"Let's play again," LC said, "and I'll show you."

"You will?" said Flex. "I can show you some trick moves for the cyborg if you want."

"Cool," said LC. "Then when we're finished you can play one of my friends."

"Okay," said Flex. He put a quarter in for LC. "I owe you one."

LC smiled. Maybe Flex wasn't such a bad critter after all.